DR. AUDREYANN C. MOSES

SILVER

MOON

By Dr. AudreyAnn C. Moses

DR. AUDREYANN C. MOSES

OTHER BOOKS BY DR. MOSES

Jane's Journey… A Journal of Transformation (2025)
The Heart Abound Novelette Series
(Book 1 of the Dead Girl Walking Trilogy)
Pa-Pro-Vi Publishing

Dead Girl Walking…What's In A Name (2023)
The Heart Abound Novelette Series
(Book 1 of the Dead Girl Walking Trilogy)
Pa-Pro-Vi Publishing

Dead Girl Walking…
New Renaissance: A Collection of African American Fiction (2022)
Edited by: Dr. Rhonda Lawson
Meet The World Image Solutions

Kelly Crews Publishing

The Heart Abound Novelette Series
The Swing (2018) (Book 1)
2nd Edition (2025) Pa-Pro-Vi Publishing

Earl Grey Chronicles
Uninvited Memories (2018) (Book 1)
A State of Affairs: Deception (2022) (Book 2)
2nd Editions (2025) Pa-Pro-Vi Publishing

Saved By Grace Series

Saved by Grace: Walking Through Affliction Into God's Deliverance (2017) (Book 1)
The Story of Wade...The Road from Darkness to Redemption (2020) (Book 2)
2nd Editions (2025) Pa-Pro-Vi Publishing

Voice of Truth Publishing

RITES OF PASSAGE:
Does It Give American Black Youths the "Right To Pass?" (2010)
(Assisted by Kenneth Nyamayaro Mufuka, Ph.D.)

ACKNOWLEDGEMENTS

I just want to say Thank You God for putting words in my head to uplift others when they feel no one cares, and no one is listening. Silver Moon is the last of a trilogy about neglect and uninvolved parenting. These books follow the life of a young lady who thought all was lost until she met a lady who knew Jesus. And once Jane started learning how Jesus was, and who she was to Him, her entire life changed.

Thank you to my husband Leonard, my children and my family and friends for never allowing me to feel I wasn't enough.

I would like to give a very special thank you to my navy shipmates, Steven McCormick, Dennis Moll, and Mark Webb, who made sure my details were realistic and factual.

Be the person who tells a stranger, a neighbor, a family member or an enemy that Jesus loves them and so do you.

Thank you to everyone willing to show love and compassion to another human just because.
Thank you to those who kept me encouraged.

Thank you Dr. LaQuita Parks and Pa-Pro-Vi Publishing for introducing my books to the world, one more time.
(https://paprovipublishing.com)

Thank you Dr. Jacquiline Cox (ClassEDefined - https://listenlindapresents1.com) for the beautiful book cover.

To God be the Glory.

<u>DEDICATION</u>

This book is dedicated to everyone who thought they were not enough until someone came along, hugged them and taught them they are more than enough, and that God put them here for a divine purpose.

This book is dedicated to EVERYONE suffering with Post Traumatic Stress Disorder. Yes, this story is about a Navy Veteran, but we know that many people not involved with the military deal with the effects of trauma and live with PTSD. Pray for them and lend a hand whenever the opportunity presents itself.

I pray the final road on Jane's miraculous journey helps you realize you are more than enough regardless of where you were born, how you were born, what you were called, or how you were treated. God loves you and He has a plan for your life.

On this day STOP allowing humans to steal your joy. Permit Him to show you how marvelous you really are.

"Blessed are the meek for they shall inherit the earth,"

(Matthew 5:5 KJV)

Table of Contents

PRELUDE

I am praying, asking God to be quick with His response. *If Hezekiah is the one for me, show me something I've never seen before.*

When I opened my eyes, there it was — the most breathtaking sunset I had ever witnessed, fiery hues melting into soft pastels. I motioned to Hezekiah to look.

He leaned against the tree beside me and quietly took my hand. We didn't speak. We didn't need to. We just stood there, letting the silence hold us as the sky surrendered to twilight.

Then, as shadows deepened and the last colors of the sun faded...

"Look at the moon," he whispered, pointing upward.

I followed his gaze. "It looks silver against the sky."

He smiled, a quiet warmth in his eyes. A *Silver Moon*.

A Whirlwind Of Thoughts...

Sometimes I stand in front of the mirror and talk to myself. Dr. Matthews says that, contrary to popular belief, it's perfectly fine to do so. Sometimes you are the only one who knows what you're going through — and the only one who can answer the question.

I'm grateful I can still talk to her and to Mrs. Johnnes. They, along with Tamera, are the anchors in my life. I truly don't know what I would have done without them.

These days, my mind is full. Our little family is growing by leaps and bounds. The children seem eager to go back to school, yet they're making the most of every ounce of summer they have left. The twins are about to start middle school. Melody and Ruth are heading into first grade. And Esther — well, she's running both houses now.

I never imagined I would have a life so full of love and excitement. Every morning, I stand on my balcony and praise God for His blessings. Two years ago, you could not have convinced me there was a God for me anywhere in the universe. And now I talk to Him like both a friend and a father. It's a wonderful feeling.

Tamera and I are planning one or two more trips to the market before our summer garden is finished. We've canned enough beans, tomatoes, cucumbers, squash, okra, and corn to make gumbo for the rest of our lives. I love hearing the children run through the market, calling out in their almost Geechee dialect, *"WA-TA-MELON! GET YA WA-TA-MELON HERE!"*

We still have berries and potatoes, and we've already started turning the soil in preparation for next year. Our winter garden is in, filled with every kind of green imaginable, plus pumpkins, butternut squash, and more beans.

It's been a great summer — one where we've fed our families and neighbors, and even made a little profit at the market. I'm already looking forward to the winter harvest and the holiday vegetables we'll have for sale. It's been the best summer of my life. Thank You, God.

Hezekiah Arnell Jackson

"Love is patient, love is kind. It does not envy, it does not boast, it is not proud."
(1 Corinthians 13:4 NIV)

Frank and Hezekiah have become Siamese twins — you don't see one without the other, especially on weekends. If one is missing, it's because he's working or out of town. I'd say it's sickening, but the truth is, I enjoy having Hezekiah around. He's been true to his word: he isn't pressing me to decide about "us," yet he makes sure I know he's serious about "us."

We've gone on dates — movies, dinner, that sort of thing. He's extremely respectful of my space, and I'm grateful. Men and women nowadays — especially my age — aren't always respectful of other people's boundaries the way they used to be back in the day. I hear young women say, "It's the '90s! If they can do it, we can do it!" Music and TV cheer them on, and some girls end up chasing boys (as Mrs. Johnnes would say) like they've got nothing better to do.

I never chased boys because I wasn't wanted. I took enough bullying as it was; I didn't need the laughter that would come with getting turned down. When a boy finally paid attention to me, I thought he was serious. I married him — and you know the rest. Bad news.

I have been ignoring God, at least as much as a sane person dares. I hear Him saying Hezekiah is the one. I hear Him saying we wouldn't be unequally yoked. I hear Him saying Hezekiah was made for me, and I for him. I hear all of this — and I'm still afraid. Afraid that if I step over that threshold, I'll lose myself.

I never understood what it meant to have confidence in myself. I never understood self-concept, self-worth, self-identity, self-esteem. My professor calls them *the four selfs*. She says you can't have one without the others, and they're either all high or all at some level of low. I've been various levels of low all my life, and now that I'm learning to regulate my "selfs," I'm afraid the stress of a relationship will push me back.

One night Tamera came up to my apartment just to see what I was doing. We sat on the balcony, sipping, and I told her how I was feeling. Having a sister to talk to is new for me, and I relish the moments we steal away for ourselves. I told her I have strong feelings for Hezekiah, but I'm scared of what might happen—so many what-ifs. She said I'd have to trust that God knows what He's doing with Hezekiah. I asked how she did it.

She said it wasn't easy. She said Frank is a lot like Hezekiah—his patience is long-suffering. She laughed and told me his spirit was courting her spirit when she wasn't even paying attention. One night she woke up and knew she couldn't live another day without him fully in her life. She called him, told him she loved him, hung up, and went back to sleep. When she woke up the next morning, he was on her stoop with coffee and a newspaper. I laughed so hard I could barely breathe. I told her I could imagine Hezekiah doing something similar — sitting under the tree.

I told her about the night we saw the silver moon — how we held hands, watched the sun set, and admired the moon laced in silver. She said she's been all over the world and has never seen a silver moon. I told her I asked God, *If You want me to be with Hezekiah, show me something I've never seen before.* He showed me the most beautiful sunset I've ever witnessed — and the silver moon.

Tamera sat straight up and looked me dead in the eyes. "Was that not the answer you wanted from God? How many different ways must God tell you that man is yours?"

She started pacing my little patio. "Or are you waiting for God to take him from you and give him to someone more deserving? Then who will you blame for your loss?"

Her voice rose. "God or Hezekiah? Neither. You'll only be able to blame yourself."

Then she sat beside me, took my face in her hands, and made sure I heard her. "God is telling you — LOUD and CLEAR — he is yours and you are his."

She held me while I cried like one of the kids when they're hurt. I told her I understood. The bad things that happened can't be changed. I can live there if I choose. But if I want better for my life and for the girls, I have to let the past stay in the past. I have to accept the blessings God has already given me. I have to accept the blessing He's trying to give me now — Hezekiah.

"I love him, Tamera. And I'm sure he loves me—but for how long?"

Tamera smiled. "How long will you keep breathing, Jane? Because that's how long I believe Hezekiah will love you."

I hugged her. "You don't think he'll still love me when I'm no longer breathing?"

She punched my arm. "Girl, stop. Go to bed. I've got to get up early tomorrow." Then she frowned. "You know my Navy days are almost over. A couple more months and I'll be retired. I don't know what I'll do with myself. What if I can't do it?"

I hugged her and told her she'll be just fine—because I'm here, and I'll help her get through it...whatever "it" is.

I watched her go down the steps, into her house, and close the door before I went back into mine. I checked on the girls and then lay across my bed. *Will anything ever be the same again?* I asked God.

No, He said.

I picked up the phone and dialed. When he answered, I said, "Hezekiah, I love you."

Then I hung up the phone and went to sleep.

Terrified Is Not A Developmental Stage...

I woke up thinking, *Oh, what a beautiful Friday morning,* until I remembered the phone call I made last night. My mood flipped instantly to, *Oh Lord, I want You to help me!*

I called him—and told him I love him. What was I thinking? He's going to think I was drunk… which, technically, I must have been, although one glass of wine doesn't usually make me do stupid things like call up a man in the middle of the night to profess my love.

Why would I do such a thing?

Okay, God, I know You had everything to do with this. So… now what? I'll probably never see him again.

Then I remembered Tamera saying Frank was sitting on her stoop. I ran to the door. Nope. Not on my steps. Not by the tree. No car in the yard.

Oh. My. Goodness. WHAT have I done? I cannot face the world today. I just… can't.

I was about to crawl back into bed when Ruth came bouncing out of her room, cheery as ever in her butterfly shirt and pants, talking about catching butterflies today with Mr. Hezekiah and Hakiem.

Oh no. No. No.

I'd forgotten. We're going to the Butterfly Exhibit at the Children's Museum today. The entire family — minus Tamera, who has to work — is going. How am I supposed to survive without her? This will be the worst day in the history of my life.

Then I heard a loud voice in my head: *"Just stop! PLEASE! Just stop! You're about to give ME a headache! Get yourself and Esther together — he'll be here in 20 minutes!"*

Okay God, You've got jokes this morning.
This is a disaster and You know it, so here's
my plan: I'll be cool, calm, and collected. I
won't say a word. I'll pretend I never called
him.

"*Whatever works for you,*" God said. "*Just
remember what I told you — he is yours, and you are
his. Enjoy the butterflies.*"

By the time Esther and I were ready, the
twins and Melody were running up my stairs
yelling for us. Ruth and Esther were already
halfway down, all five children chattering at
the top of their lungs about how many
butterflies they'd see today. I still don't
understand how they can all talk at once and
still know exactly what the others are saying.
It's a talent.

I decided on a yellow summer dress,
white tennis shoes, and a white hat with a
butterfly sash. Perfect for the day. Just as I
stepped outside, I spotted Frank and Hezekiah

talking under the tree. His back was to me, so I felt safe—until Frank did that chin-jerk thing men do to signal each other.

Hezekiah turned just as the girls swarmed me, squealing about my dress and demanding one just like it. Out of the corner of my eye, I saw both men taking pictures.

God.

Hezekiah came over, hand extended to help me down the last steps, the girls still wrapped around my legs. Off to the side, the boys muttered about being glad they weren't girls—"all that noise"—until James announced, with his hand rubbing his invisible beard, he wanted to be "smooth like Mr. Hezekiah!" John nodded solemnly, also rubbing his invisible beard, "Oh yeah. Smooth." Then came the laughter.

When I looked back, Hezekiah was still holding my hand, studying my face like he was searching for an answer my mouth wouldn't give — again.

"Is it true?" he asked.

"Yes," I said softly.

I could have fallen right into his smile and never come out.

He pulled me closer. "Please... tell me again."

I leaned in so my lips brushed his ear, and my spirit spoke to his spirit. "I love you."

I straightened, smiled, and tried to walk toward the car, but he didn't let go. Then he turned to Frank and shouted, "IT'S TRUE!"

Frank gave him two thumbs up, the girls danced as if they knew exactly what was going on, and the boys rolled their eyes in unison, silently declaring, "*Mr. Hezekiah... you just lost your smooth.*"

I smiled. *Okay God, it's all up to You now. I don't know what real love feels or looks like, but You keep telling me Hezekiah is mine and I am his.*

I'm taking Your word for it and looking forward, not back. Still, I have to depend on You – and I pray You keep up Your end of the deal. That's all. I'm not saying amen, because this conversation isn't over.

Everyone was already in the car. After Esther was born, Frank bought a new SUV during the New Year sales and gave me his old one – perfect for me and the girls. He taught me to drive it, helped me get my permit and license, and kept the bigger vehicle for himself – a beautiful Nissan Pathfinder. Ten seats. Perfect for boosters and car seats. The boys always head for the back, claiming it as their private space.

The day at the museum was wonderful. The Butterfly Exhibit was breathtaking. The best part of having young children is getting to do all the things I missed in my own childhood. I always thank God for that gift.

By the time we got home, everyone was exhausted. The children fell asleep quickly. Tomorrow, when Tamera gets home, they'll wake up ready to relive every detail, proudly giving her the butterfly crafts they made.

It was a good day.

When The Terror Lingers...

"He healeth the broken in heart, and bindeth up their wounds."--Psalm 147:3 KJV

Hezekiah sat in his "classroom," which was really an auto mechanic's bay big enough to hold three 18-wheeler trucks, each with their insides scattered across the floor. It was the students' job to put them back together again.

The old Humpty Dumpty rhyme rolled through his mind, and he shook his head with a faint smile. Why had he decided to become a mechanic? He'd been doing just fine as a driver—the pay was good, the travel steady.

But driving had cost him time with his son. And then there was Hakeem. After their father walked out, Hezekiah felt it was his responsibility to help his sister raise the boy. Their father couldn't bear the guilt of being the cause of Hakeem's disability. Even after Hakeem told him, "I don't hold it against you. You'll always be my dad — just call," the man still left.

Those were good enough reasons to change careers — but not the real one.

The real reason was the day his life split into *before* and *after*.

While serving in the Navy, Hezekiah had sustained life-threatening injuries and witnessed the horrific death of a sailor in the ship's boiler room. A pipe burst without warning, releasing a blast of scalding steam that killed the man instantly. Hezekiah was close enough to see it happen — close enough to smell the burn, hear the screams, feel the heat. Close enough that he didn't realize he'd been burned too, not until other sailors pulled him out.

The ship's medical team quickly saw that his breathing was labored and that his arms and legs had been burned. He was medevac'd off the ship — conscious, but numb to the pain, deaf to everything except the screams echoing in his mind.

The incident was officially ruled an accident, and it truly was, but the personnel responsible for maintaining the equipment was cleared of any wrongdoing. That part hurt almost as much as the loss itself.

Months of physical recovery followed, but emotionally, he was falling apart. Every whistle from a pipe, every creak of metal, even the hiss of a coffee pot sent him into panic. The panic continued into his sleep as he began to experience night terrors - hearing the screams, experiencing the smell of scalding skin and fumes from the boiler.

When he was finally allowed back aboard, he couldn't perform his boiler room duties. He was reassigned to shore duty, but the trauma followed him there. After nearly two years of evaluations, the Navy decided he could no longer safely perform his duties. On the recommendation of military mental health staff, Hezekiah was honorably discharged with full benefits under a medical separation for PTSD.

Civilian life gave him space, but not healing — not at first. Pain was a constant companion, sometimes real, sometimes imagined. He relied on medication and drank more cognac than he should have, sliding into opioid addiction. Flashbacks still came — triggered by certain sounds, smells, even a cloud of steam from a kitchen pot.

Progress came, but slowly. Too slow to save his marriage. Too slow to erase the loss of the only job he'd ever loved. He stuck with therapy and joined both PTSD and substance abuse support groups, trying to rebuild.

Eventually, after the divorce, he relocated to Beaufort, South Carolina. Through a veteran program, he was offered training as an 18-wheeler driver. It wasn't on his "five-things-I-want-to-be-when-I-grow-up" list, but to his surprise, he took to it. He loved the freedom of the road, the rhythm of the highways, the quiet solitude between towns.

For a while, he even found joy again—until the day the past came roaring back.

He was driving I-95 about twenty miles outside Beaufort when it happened. A high-pitched whistle escaped from the rig, followed by a burst of steam through the dashboard vents—thick, hot, and far too familiar.

His chest locked. In a heartbeat, he was back in the ship's belly: metal groaning, men shouting, steam peeling skin.

By the grace of God, he didn't lose control. Hands trembling, heart pounding, he guided the truck to the shoulder. He sat there, stunned, trying to piece together where he was. The cab was still fogging with steam. He patted his arms, touched his face—no burns.

He can't remember how long he sat in the cab, probably only seconds, but it seemed like hours. He climb from the cab, again checking his body for burns. He called dispatch. Blue lights pulled up behind him while he was still trying to explain—to them, and to himself—what just happened.

The next day, the company's mechanic found the cause: a failed water pump had overheated the engine. A coolant hose had burst, spraying superheated fluid and filling the cab with steam. Logical explanation. But the damage was already done.

That night, the nightmares came back. Only this time, the boiler room and the truck blurred into one scene. The whistle, the hiss, the smell—they all collided. He woke drenched in sweat.

The next morning, he saw his therapist, who helped him separate the two events and ground himself in the present. But he didn't drive for two weeks.

When he finally returned, fear rode shotgun. He drove slower, stuck to the outside lane, stopped more often. It became obvious — he couldn't keep doing this.

He went to Antonio, the company's owner — a fellow veteran who already knew about the boiler room and the PTSD. Together, they agreed it was time for Hezekiah to step away from the driver's seat.

But he didn't want to leave the work he'd grown to love. He shifted to dispatch for a while. Then one day, watching the shop mechanics work on a diesel engine, something clicked.

He didn't want to drive the trucks anymore.

He wanted to fix them.

And more than that—he wanted to keep people safe.

In All My Ways...

"...in all my ways submit to Him, and He will make my paths straight".
(Proverbs 3:6 NIV)"

We've made it a habit to take the children to church whenever possible. We split up the month so there's always an adult to go with them — whether it's children's church worship service, choir practice, or whatever else they're involved in.

Frank, Tamera, and I haven't committed ourselves to a specific church. We each have our own relationship with God... and of course, I still have my "Jesus papers" from Mrs. Johnnes. I keep them on the coffee table now — Frank and Tamera have been reading them. James read one the other day and asked a thousand questions. I finally handed him Mrs. Johnnes' phone number and said, "Call your Granny. She's got all the answers."

Today, we got a little break. The children's choir isn't singing, and they asked to sleep in and just go to the evening youth program. I didn't protest.

My mind feels heavy — too much on it. Exams are coming up. Tamera's retiring from the Navy soon. And then there's the heaviest weight of all: Hezekiah.

I know the scripture — trust in the Lord with all my heart, mind, and soul — but right now, the wrong voices are chattering in my head. As happy as I was yesterday with him, today those voices tell me I'm not worthy of a good man.

I thought about calling Mrs. Johnnes so she could pray these voices away, but I could hear her in my mind: *"Child, pray the scriptures. When you're overwhelmed… pray the scriptures. Don't try to come up with your own words — just pray the scriptures."*

I checked to make sure the children were still asleep, then picked up my Bible and went to the patio outside my bedroom. I sat down talking to God, "I don't know which scriptures to pray?" I opened my Bible — it fell open to Proverbs chapter 3, *Wisdom Bestows Well-Being.*

I began reading, inserting myself into the verses:

"Jane, do not forget My teaching, but keep My commands in your heart, for they will prolong your life many years and bring you peace and prosperity. Jane, let love and faithfulness never leave you; bind them around your neck. Lord, please write them on the tablet of my heart, so I win favor and a good name in Your sight — and in the sight of man. I will trust in the Lord with all my heart and lean not on my own understanding; in all my ways I will submit to Him, and He will make my paths straight." Amen.

As I continued reading, I thought of the faith reminders God had given me through Dr. Matthews, Mrs. Johnnes, and now Tamera. Even though I've been asking God for wisdom and understanding, I haven't been fully open to His responses—especially when it comes to Hezekiah.

I want to give myself to him. I want to be vulnerable. But men still remind me of the mistreatment I endured as a child and as a wife. How can I risk that again?

My eyes fell on verse 15: *"She is more precious than rubies; nothing you desire can compare with her."*

I froze. These were the exact words Hezekiah had said to me the other day. Word for word.

I'd asked him why he wanted to be with me when I was clearly not ready. I told him I knew I loved him—but how was I supposed to separate "a man" from "the men" who had abused me? My goal in coming to Beaufort was to reunite with my sister, get on my feet, and build a better life for my daughters. I wasn't looking for a man—certainly not before I was wise enough to discern if he was the right one for me.

He told me there was an old proverb about wisdom—how those who find it are blessed, and how it's more valuable than silver or gold. He said when he first heard it, it was about becoming wealthy, but a wise friend had told him it also meant he should look for a woman who listens to the counsel of God. She would be more precious than gold or rubies.

As his words replayed in my mind, I asked God why it was so important I be with Hezekiah. Why should I trust him? I'd trusted before, and look how that turned out.

Sometimes the Holy Spirit speaks in that still, small voice. Sometimes it's like thunder.

But this morning—nothing. No words. No song. Just silence.

I must have dozed off because I felt little fingers in my hair.

"Mommy, when are you gonna get your hair done? It's time."

"Yes ma'am, Momma Ruth, I'll make an appointment."

We both laughed. She loves it when I call her that—probably because she's always telling me what I should or shouldn't be doing.

Still smoothing my hair, she said, "You should let me put it in a pretty style for when Mr. Hezekiah comes over. You want to look pretty for Mr. Hezekiah, don't you?"

Before I could answer, she kept going: "I know you like him! Well, don't you? I know he likes you! I can tell by the way he looks at you and the way he held your hand all day. They don't hold your hand like that if they don't like you." She collapsed into my arms laughing like it was the funniest thing she'd ever said.

"You're five. What do you know about holding hands?" I asked, laughing with her.

For a fleeting second, I thought about how my mother and I never laughed together. Ever. How sad. I forced my mind back to the joy of this moment — I never want to forget what it feels like.

A voice from the stairs made us stop.

"Auntie Tamera, guess what! Mommy's got a boyfriend!" Ruth shouted. From behind Tamera, Melody's voice rang out in confirmation: "Yep!" The two girls ran into the house laughing hysterically.

Tamera looked from the doorway to me. "What happened while I was off defending the country against enemies foreign and domestic?"

I shrugged, forgetting there were still tiny yellow feathers floating around my mouth.

Tamera laughed and sat down. "This is gonna be good. Spit it out, young lady. Why do our daughters think you have a boyfriend all of a sudden? The other night you weren't listening to God or anybody else."

She gave me that look—the one that says, *I already know what you did. I just want to hear you say it.*

I took a deep breath, a long swig of warm water, looked her in the eye, and said, "Well... you see, it was like this..."

God...THIS IS NOT FUNNY!

"But I tell you, love your enemies and pray for
those who persecute you, that you may be children
of your Father in heaven. He causes his sun to rise
on the evil and the good and sends rain on the
righteous and the unrighteous."
(Matthew 5:44-45 NIV)

I got a letter from my ex-husband today.

Honestly, I'd hoped that once I signed
the divorce papers, I'd never hear from him
again. I knew that was impossible — we have
children — but still, a woman can hope.

Apparently, he'd left a note on Mrs.
Johnnes' door, asking her to forward his new
address to me. With a little nudging from her, I
wrote him a quick letter, told him about the
girls, and sent a few pictures so he could see
how much Ruth has grown and meet Esther
for the first time… on paper.

I struggled to do even that much. This is
the man who dumped our girls on the side of

the road and refused to even acknowledge Esther's birth. But, since I'm trying to be a grown-up *and* a Christian, I figured doing the bare minimum was still better than throwing his note straight in the trash.

Today, I received a letter from him

"Dear Jane,

Thank you so much for sending me the pictures of the girls. You're doing a great job raising them – they're beautiful. I doubt Ruth remembers me except for what you've told her. I don't think you have any pictures of me, and I don't remember ever taking any except when we got married. That's my fault.

Hopefully, one day you'll let me see them… get to know them.

I'm doing good under the circumstances. I'm glad the Jesus Papers Lady forwarded you my new address. I'm in a boarding halfway house. When I got into trouble, they put me in a program that will last a couple of years. That's fine – I did bad things to you and against you. I took my anger over things that had nothing to do with you out on you and Ruth. I don't deserve forgiveness, but I hope you'll give it one day. I'd like it if you'd keep writing – let me know how the girls are… and how you are.

In your letter, you didn't tell me anything about yourself. How do you like Beaufort? How's it going with your sister? I remember you saying she left when you were very young, so I was surprised to read you decided to live with her. I can understand if you feel I don't deserve to know anything about you. Maybe you're right. But I thought I'd ask anyway.

There's a part of me that knows I've burned bridges between us that can't be rebuilt. Still… I'm hoping there's a chance – once I get myself together – for us. I'll be in this program for a couple of years, so you have time to decide. Maybe you'll even want to move back to New Orleans. Who knows?

I know you can't bring the girls to see me here, but I'm talking to them about moving me to the Beaufort area — closer to you and the girls. Would that be something you'd agree with?

I've been taking classes to get back into college. I've been doing anger management and talking to a therapist whenever I can. I know it's a lot to think about.

Take care of yourself. I'll write again and send a picture of me for the girls as soon as soon as I can.

Love for you and the girls,

Tim"

I sat at the table, staring at the letter. I wanted to say something to God about it, but the only things that came to mind weren't very nice — so I kept those thoughts to myself.

My brain was spinning.

So God… what exactly do You want me to do now?

He divorced me. He divorced me and these girls without hesitation. When he was with us, he was abusive and mean — and now I'm supposed to believe he's changed because of this letter? Is that what You're telling me?

This much change… in *this* short a time? I don't know. I really doubt it.

Am I reading this right? He wants me to keep writing to him? He wants me to bring the girls to see him? He wants me to send him pictures of *me*? He wants us to "work on getting back together"?!

Does he actually think I still love him? Or that I want him to love me? Is that what's in his head?

Is he crazy, or am I crazy? Which one is it?

The anger tears were already rising. There has never been love for me in that man's body. And I can't believe he truly loves these girls either.

So what now?

Well, I know what I'm *not* going to do.

I'm not writing him back — not right now. And I am not considering getting back together. EVER.

We're divorced. He didn't care then. He's had sex all over the place — who knows where, who knows with whom — including Samantha. Maybe I should just tell him to call *her*.

God, I don't need or want him in my life — especially now that I've fallen in love with Hezekiah.

Wait... did You *tell* him to give his address to Mrs. Johnnes just so he could pop back into my life? Because I don't understand this. You nudged me toward Hezekiah, and now Tim's writing like we're supposed to reunite?

Is there some lesson here I'm not getting?

Ah. I see it now. I've heard of this before — men get into church or some 12-step program and are told to "reconcile" with their ex-wives. Some of them even become Christians and suddenly remember how good their wives were. Then they start with the "I've changed, I'm different now" speeches.

And in Tim's case? It would last just long enough to get me to believe him. Just long enough to remarry me. Just long enough to get me pregnant again. And then — BOOM — he'd be back to his old self.

And you know whose fault that would be, God?

Mine.

God, I know I haven't exactly given You room to speak here… but I hope You'll shine a little light on this. Is there a Jesus Paper I haven't read yet that deals with *this* kind of mess?

I probably need to call Mrs. Johnnes and Dr. Matthews to help me sort this out. But not today.

I'll wait and see what You come up with.

Right now, I'm going to make a glass of iced tea and walk in the garden. I need to de-stress.

This feels like the perfect day to pull weeds.

Thank You very much.

It's Time....

"The plans of the heart belong to man; But the answer of the tongue is from Jehovah." (Proverbs 16:1 ASV)

When I'm stressed, I sometimes hear Mrs. Johnnes hum-singing a familiar old song around the house:

"I don't feel no ways tired. I come too far from where I started from. Nobody told me the road would be easy, and I don't believe He brought me this far to leave me."

It's been a week since I got Tim's letter. I haven't had time — or maybe just haven't wanted — to think much about him or it. I didn't mention it to Tamera; she's busy getting ready for her retirement.

I've been studying for final exams, helping Melody and Ruth with homework, and working with Tamera on creating a winter garden — tilling, fertilizing, and prepping our plot. Fun, fun, fun. No time for Tim's shenanigans.

I haven't spent much time with Hezekiah lately, though he hasn't been far away. He still hangs out with Frank and the boys — coaching Little League and other male-only activities. We've talked on the phone, and he says things like, "School and work are kicking my butt," or "I miss you," or "I've got a few things to work out." I say similar things back. Then we hang up. I'm not going to stress myself wondering about his "things" because my stress level is already at its peak.

When I spoke separately to Mrs. Johnnes and Dr. Matthews about Tim, they both pointed out something interesting — this is the first time I've called him by name - ever. They were right. That's sad.

I told them no amount of becoming a Christian — on his part or mine — would make me take him back. He's done terrible things to me, and I won't relive that pain again. He pretended to love me and want to be with me forever and always. Maybe he wanted a wife forever, but he didn't want a *partner*—someone to devote his heart and soul to.

What he wanted was a live-in cook, housekeeper, baby factory, and punching bag when he got frustrated, while he ran the streets with any woman he got drunk with.

I cannot go back there. I will not go back there. I cannot imagine God would want that life for me again.

Mrs. Johnnes reminded me that I don't know whether he's trying to change or not, and that the Bible says not to judge without the facts. I told her, "Paul said the only one who knows the thoughts of a man is the spirit in that man—and I don't believe the spirit in Tim has any good intentions at all!"

I could almost hear her smiling. "I see you've been studying. That makes me happy, daughter. Now let's finish that scripture. What else did Paul say?"

Almost whispering, I replied, "The rest says no one knows God's thoughts except the Spirit of God." (1 Corinthians 2:13, paraphrased)

"But Mrs. Johnnes, you can't possibly think I should consider giving him a second chance!"

"No, baby. I'm saying we don't know God's plans for you or for him. God is trying to save both of you. Who's to say He hasn't put you where you are so you can introduce Tim to Him?"

I whimpered, "For such a time as this… like Queen Esther."

Tears came—partly from guilt for not considering that Tim might be worth saving in

God's eyes, even if not in mine. And partly from being upset with her for reminding me.

"Daughter, don't cry. I know you're scared and confused right now. I also know you've got Hezekiah on your mind, wondering what God was thinking that day he helped you in the hallway. Remember—God is passionate and loving. He won't put more on you than you can bear. That means He knows you'll think this through, pray about it, and ask Him what He wants you to do. I believe everything will work out the way it should... for you, for Hezekiah, and for Tim."

By the end of that call, I had a full-blown migraine. I laid down, fell asleep, and woke disoriented when something startled me.

It was Tamera, just about to unlock the door with her key when I opened it.

"Girl, what is going on with you!? I've been calling forever!" she half-screeched.

I winced, holding my head. "Please stop yelling! My head is killing me — don't make it worse."

She touched my forehead, speaking more quietly. "What's wrong with you? We were supposed to go shopping an hour ago. I waited, I called, and when you didn't answer, I came up here."

I picked up Tim's letter from where I'd left it and handed it to her. When she saw who it was from, she rolled her eyes.

After reading it, she gave me that big-sister *what-exactly-is-going-on-here* frown. I handed her a cup of spiced tea. She sipped, silent for a long moment, then re-read certain parts.

"What does he mean by 'talk about us'?" she asked. "And why would he think it's okay to say he wants to move to Beaufort to be near you and the girls?"

I shrugged. "I don't know. Maybe because he's in some kind of recovery program, he thinks I'd feel safe with him now."

Tamera paced the floor, then stopped abruptly. "So why do you have a migraine? This is ridiculous, but it's not migraine-worthy. Are you actually considering taking him back? Are you thinking about going back to New Orleans? YOU BETTER NOT BE!"

I almost said some very unholy words. "WHAT?! Girl, no! Have you lost your mind?!"

Now I was pacing, telling her about my conversations with Dr. Matthews and Mrs. Johnnes.

"It was Mrs. Johnnes that gave me the headache. She wasn't telling me to go back to him—just saying maybe, 'What would Jesus do.'"

Tamera, sipping her tea again, frowned. "What's that supposed to mean? The man's a maniac! Is she trying to say God might have gotten through to him or something?"

I laughed. "I think she's saying I should pray and ask God what to do."

We sat in silence, unsure what to say next. Then Tamera smacked her forehead. "Girl, I forgot to tell you — Hezekiah's in the barn with Frank and the boys. He asked for you... again. Sorry, when you showed me the letter, I forgot."

I started crying — hard. Tamera rushed over, hugged me, and rocked me like one of the girls with a scraped knee. I couldn't stop. Couldn't talk. Could barely breathe.

She grabbed her phone and called Frank. "Send Hezekiah up here."

I heard Frank asking what was wrong, and Tamera saying, "Just send him."

I told her no — I didn't want to see him. She said yes, it was time. Time to tell him what my life had really been like — not the sugarcoated version I'd been giving him.

"It's time," she said.

He answers in a prayer...

But the answer of the tongue is from Jehovah."

(Proverbs 16:1 ASV)

Within moments of Tamera's call, I heard what sounded like horses stampeding up the stairs. I had pulled myself together enough to stop the hard crying. Tamera and I looked at each other and shook our heads.

"Did I say you were bleeding or something?" she asked.

"I don't think so," I replied.

We both laughed just as they burst through the door — Hezekiah, Frank, James, John, and one of the dogs. Tamera hugged me, kissed my cheek, and then promptly herded everyone back out, with the exception of Hezekiah. I could hear them protesting as they clambered back down the stairs.

I stood and told him I'd made some spiced tea. I took the long way around the couch to the kitchen so I wouldn't have to pass close enough for him to touch me. I knew if he did, I'd fall apart.

"Thank you," he said, watching me closely. He didn't move from his spot, just kept his eyes on me like it was his job to keep me in sight.

When I returned with a tray of tea, cups, honey, spoons, and the lemon squares I'd baked, he still didn't touch me — not even to take the tray. He just watched.

I set it on the coffee table. "Would you like to sit here?" I patted the couch beside me. "Or over there?"

He chose the chair closest to the couch but not the couch itself. Later, he told me he could see I was holding myself together by a thread. If he'd sat next to me, he would have wanted to hold me — and he wasn't sure if that's what I needed.

We sat in silence. I sipped tea; he watched me sip tea. Finally, I asked if he was ready for finals.

"As ready as an old brain can be," he said.

"What about you", he asked, "Are you ready?"

I smiled. "As ready as a weary brain can be," I answered — instantly regretting it. The tears welled again, and I closed my eyes to keep them from spilling.

He moved to the couch beside me. "What's going on, Jane? I know you've been working through some things — so have I. But this feels different. Something happened. What happened?"

The flood refused to be held back. I handed him the letter, wiping at my eyes before the tears fell. I watched his expression shift—curiosity, confusion, something like pity. He shook his head as he read the end.

When he finally looked at me, his eyes were soft, questioning. He poured himself another cup of tea, head bent just enough that I couldn't see his eyes.

I prayed silently, asking God what to do—and how to properly chastise Tamera for putting me in this situation.

"Is he the reason you've been struggling to commit to me?" His voice was low, steady. "Because of what he did to you in New Orleans?"

"Yes," I said, my voice barely above a whisper. "That... and the family strife. I told you some things, but not everything."

"Are you ready to tell me everything now?"

So I did.

I told him the story of Janedoah—of being neglected and abused from birth. Of the

Mardi Gras float. Of meeting Mrs. Johnnes and Dr. Matthews. Of how Esther was conceived. Of Tamera.

Once I started, I couldn't stop. Words and tears poured out until there were no more words, only tears and silence.

Hezekiah's eyes were wet, pain written across his face. I reached for a napkin, but before I could, he set the letter down and pulled me into his arms. His body trembled — whether from anger, sadness, or both, I couldn't tell. He stroked my hair, kissed my forehead.

"Shhh... you're with me now. You're safe," he murmured. "I prayed for the right answers, and the only answer I got was this — God will help me keep you safe. I'll help you be happy and prosperous, but only if you let me."

He gently tilted my face so I had to meet his eyes. "I love you. He doesn't. I want to be your priest, your provider, your protector, your lover, your confidant. He doesn't. I want to be a father to Ruth and Esther. He doesn't. But it's up to you to decide if I'm capable — if I'm worthy of your trust."

I wiped the tears from his face. "I was afraid you'd be angry about the letter. About me writing him in the first place. I only thought it would be good for him to have pictures of the girls. I didn't expect him to think I wanted him back. Even without you, I would never go back to him."

"Shhh. God erased the idea that you might go back. He told me Tim was never the one you were supposed to be with. God untangles the messes we make so that, if we choose, we end up where we should be — with who we should be with. I don't know how you and I would have met before you went into labor with Esther, and I don't plan to dwell on it. All I know is I love you — and I need you to love me back. But you can't fully love me until you know my story. So... let's order food, ask Tamera to watch the girls, and talk. Is that okay?"

I nodded and rested against his chest.

God, I hope You know what You're doing.

While we ate he told me his story. His childhood, the trouble he'd gotten into with the law, his marriage to his high school sweetheart who he later found out had lied about being pregnant with his child, leaving him to raise a son that wasn't even his. He told me about the accident on his ship, how it left him with post-traumatic stress disorder, and that it's the reason he wears long sleeves even in the summer. Then, for the first time, he rolled them up and showed me the scars on his arms, told me about the ones on his chest and legs. I'd never seen them before.

My heart twisted. I didn't see ugly marks — I saw battles survived. I wanted to take his hands in mine, lay my cheek against his arm, and tell him how proud I was that he was still here. Every line, every scar, felt like part of the man I had fallen so deeply in love with.

He told me how he got the job with MMTrucking through a veteran's program, and how he drove big trucks for them until just a couple months before we met.

When he described his ex's betrayal, my inside voice slipped out: "Thank God she was stupid."

His smile told me he'd heard.

"I'm sorry — that was a stupid thing to say."

He laughed. "No, you're okay. It's not a stupid question, and you're not the first one to use those kinds of words to describe her. I raised Josiah as my own even though I knew he wasn't. When he found out, it was hard on him. His mother and I had been separated for three years before we divorced. We divorced when he was thirteen and David was eight — mainly because I was struggling with PTSD and addiction, and I couldn't support her the way she wanted once I was medically separated from the Navy. She didn't want to help me, physically or emotionally.

"She got full custody of both boys. But on the divorce papers, she put that I wasn't Josiah's biological father. I was so angry with her. She tried to sever the relationship between Josiah and me, but I made sure he knew I needed him to be my son, no matter what the paperwork said.

"And since she was so spiteful as to put in writing that he wasn't mine, the judge made her pay back half the child support I'd given her while we were separated. I had them put it in a trust for him. When he gets out of college, he'll be a millionaire."

He laughed again. "Good always comes after bad."

Then he looked at me. "Like this. If you'd just marry me, can't you see how happy we'd be? The girls would have two big brothers, a father who loves them more than life, and you'd have a husband who would never leave you or mistreat you. Jane... can you feel that in your spirit, even a little?"

Tears again.

"Okay God, what is with these tears! I have not cried this much, ever. I don't think I've ever had a real reason to cry, until now. Is that your answer? Is your answer that this man is worth crying for, good, bad or indifferent? Is that what you are saying?"

I pulled back to look at him.

"Yes," I said. "Yes, I feel it in my spirit every day. I missed you when you weren't here, and when you were, I wanted to run because I couldn't fathom a man loving me for real—for me. But here you are. Patient. Giving me space. God's been trying to tell me something all along. It took that letter to shake me, to make me realize I was telling myself I didn't deserve better. When the letter came, I wanted to call you, but I thought you'd use it as a reason to leave. When Tamera called you and I heard you coming up those stairs, part of me knew you were coming for me. And the scared part disappeared when I saw you. I would marry you right now if there was a preacher here, and I would live the rest of my life thanking you for being you and lifting me up out of the muck. I love you."

He kissed me so quickly I almost didn't have enough air to handle it! Then he did something I was not expecting.

He moved the coffee table, got down on his bad knee, "I have been carrying this in my pocket for three weeks, praying for the right moment. Jane Smith Burton, will you marry me?"

In his hand was the ring Tamera and I had admired in the antique shop weeks ago.

Tears, again — for both of us. I slid to the floor with him.

"Yes, Hezekiah Jackson, I will marry you and love you forever and always."

She Said Yes...

"He who finds a wife finds a good thing and obtains favor from the Lord. (Proverbs 18:22 ESV)"

Hezekiah and Frank

"Frank, man... she said YES! Finally!"

Hezekiah was practically glowing.

"That ex of hers did me the best favor he could've ever done. I might have to shake his hand if I ever see him."

Frank laughed. "Congratulations, man. I'm happy for you. You two are going to do well together. God is good, as they say at church."

"I'm guessing you haven't talked dates yet," Frank added, chuckling. "You know how it goes — the women will make all the plans and just tell us where to be and when."

Hezekiah laughed with him. "I don't care, as long as it's not too far off. We didn't talk about it. We both have exams coming up,

and my original plan was to study last night...
but God had other plans. Hopefully, He's
planned how I'm going to ace this final, too."

He smiled softly. "I didn't stay. I didn't
want to mess up the moment. Once I saw she
was stable and okay, I left. She called this
morning to tell me she was going to show her
sister the ring."

He grinned. "I took it to mean she didn't
change her mind after I left. Praise God."

Looking at his friend seriously,
Hezekiah said, "Frank, I'd always thought I'd
ask you to be my best man. I hope you won't
mind that I plan to ask my son, Josiah, to be
my Best Man. I'd love for James, John, and my
youngest, David, to be my groomsmen."

Frank beamed. "I'm crushed! Naw,
man, I understand. And I know the boys will
be ecstatic. Honestly, I think I'd like to walk
Jane down the aisle—if she wants me to."

"I'm pretty sure she would want you to," Hezekiah said with a smile.

Jane and Tamera

As soon as I got dressed, I ran down the stairs and burst through Tamera's kitchen door—probably just as loud as the men had been the night before.

I held my hand right in front of her face. "I said YES!"

Tamera gently pulled my hand down, a big smile spreading across her face. "Jane, it's about time," she laughed. "I was about to say yes for you!"

She hugged me tight, kissing my cheeks. "I'm so happy for you, Sissy. You deserve a good man who'll treat you like the queen you are. Hezekiah is that man. He loves you—and those girls—with every ounce of blood in his body. The only way he'll leave you is if he dies... and even then, he won't be far."

"I feel the same way," I whispered. "I think I've always felt this way. I was just afraid. Not anymore."

"Are the kids already gone to school?" I asked, glancing at the clock. "I've got to go soon. Two exams today. I'm praying I studied enough, because by the time Hezekiah left last night, I was exhausted and too wired to read another word. And NO, ma'am... he did *not* spend the night!"

We both cracked up laughing.

Then Tamera looked at me with that soft, moved expression she gets when she's deeply touched. "I haven't seen you glow like this... ever."

I nodded slowly. "Tamera, every day I praise God you brought me here. I tell Him — even though He already knows — I'm certain I'd be dead if you hadn't sent for me. You've been my guardian angel this whole time.

"And now... here we are. Celebrating a whole new chapter in my life, one that never would've happened if I hadn't come. I love you so much. Not just because of Hezekiah— but because you opened your heart to a stranger and let me be your sister.

"I want you to be my Matron of Honor. And I want the girls to be my flower girl and my Maids of Honor. I love you so much."

Tamera, standing there with a dish towel in one hand and big rollers in her hair, cried like a little girl. I cried with her.

When she could finally speak, she said something I never thought I'd hear.

"Jane, I told you when you first came, I tried my best to shield you from the mess. I loved you from the moment you were born. I was the only one who refused to call you Janedoah—especially after I found out what that awful name really meant.

"I don't know if you remember me calling you 'Sissy.' That's what I used to call you."

Through tears, I nodded. "I remember — especially after hearing you say it a couple times since we've been here. I remember. There were nights I'd cry myself to sleep after Tim hit me. I would call one of the others, but they didn't care. I didn't know how to call you and I'd pray God would let you call me. I always knew you didn't treat me like the others. I remember."

Tamera smiled. "After I joined the Navy, there were times I didn't even know if you were alive. Samantha and our mother weren't any help. I tried to find you. I sent a letter — it came back marked 'no forwarding address.' I sent another — it never came back, but I never heard from you. I figured he trashed it.

"I didn't stop trying. I knew if I could just reach you, I'd take you and Ruth away from him. When I finally got in touch with you, I praised God you were still alive. Frank and I had already built the apartment, hoping and praying you'd agree to come."

By now, we were sitting at the table, crying more tears, holding on to each other like a tornado might come any minute and snatch one of us away.

Tamera continued softly, "We had no idea how it would go, having you and the girls here. We didn't know if we'd get along or how the pieces would fit. All I knew was I needed you just as much as you needed me. My life is forever changed, because I've got my Sissy back.

"So YES. I'm overwhelmed with joy to be your sister. And YES. I'd be honored to be your Matron of Honor. And I know the girls will be beside themselves."

She smiled through fresh tears. "Let's plan a wedding... after your exams."

We laughed and hugged again — this time holding on just a little longer.

Graduation Days

I've had many good days in the last few years — watching my girls grow up on a farm, knowing they are loved and safe. I never imagined so many people would pour into me daily, helping me pour into my girls.

I've learned so much about life from Tamera and Frank. Mrs. Johnnes continues to teach me about God's love for me and my daughters. Dr. Matthews reminds me often that for others to recognize my worth, I first have to recognize and validate my own.

Today was one of those days when I truly allowed myself to see my own value.

Today, I graduated from college with my Associate of Science Degree in Early Care and Education. From here, I can begin working toward my dream — starting my own daycare center and continuing my education toward a

Bachelor's Degree in Early Childhood Education.

Today is special because I reached a goal I never thought I could attain. Not because I was being held back by my ex-husband — because I allowed him to hold me back. I allowed him and others to convince me I wasn't good enough.

But today, I recognize I have always been worthy. And my goal in life is to teach my girls — and other children — that they are valuable to themselves and to God.

It was also an extraordinary day because Mrs. Johnnes and Dr. Matthews came to celebrate. But the biggest surprise was seeing my mother and sister, Samantha. Today was the first time either of them has celebrated anything with me. I didn't expect them to be there, and it made me feel warm inside to see them in the audience.

This celebration was for Hezekiah, too. His department graduated yesterday. His sons were there to cheer him on, and he was surprised to see his boss, Antonio Martin, his wife Lizanne, and several co-workers attend the ceremony. He told me Antonio had been recovering from a serious illness, so he was deeply moved to see him there. It's comforting to know there are people in the world who truly care.

The children might have enjoyed the festivities more than any of us. For both ceremonies, Tamera dressed them in T-shirts with a picture of Hezekiah and me wearing our graduation caps. She had matching shirts made for the adults and for Hezekiah's sons. We wore them both nights, and — shockingly — the girls managed to stay clean!

It was a wonderful week of celebration. And yes — everyone wanted to see the ring and talk about wedding and honeymoon plans.

Hezekiah joked about us going to the local Super 8 — "where they keep the lights on for us!" Everyone laughed. The kids suggested Disney World, and we might just take them up on that, since neither of us has been.

As I look back over these last few weeks, all I can say is Thank You, Lord, for one more beautiful day.

"Lord my God, you have done many amazing things!

You have made great plans for us — too many to list.

I could talk on and on about them,

because there are too many to count."

(Psalms 40:5 ERV)

Happy Confusion

I have never planned a wedding, been in a wedding party, or even attended a wedding—ever. And yet, here I am... planning the wedding of the century.

Hezekiah wanted to just go to the courthouse. But when I explained that I needed this experience—planning, celebrating, and being the Queen of the Ball—he conceded. His only condition was that it couldn't be next year.

He smiled that smile and said, "Sweetheart, I want to marry you today. Please don't make me wait too long. I don't want to be forty-two..."

I smiled back. "How about Sunday, December 10, 2000? That's three weeks before you turn forty-one. Is that soon enough for you to get your suit ready and your assignments done?"

"Yes, ma'am!" he laughed, swinging me around the room.

And so began the follies of wedding planning.

In the middle of it all, the children started school in August. James and John entered middle school. Melody and Ruth stayed in grade school. Esther began daycare.

It's hard watching them grow so fast. There's a bittersweetness to it — a little sadness — because I know they'll be living their own lives before I'm ready to let go. So I make sure we always have something going on, something that keeps us close and present in each other's lives.

We're also planning Tamera's retirement, set for October 30, 2000. Tamera insists her part is easy — the Navy counselor at her command is handling most of the arrangements. All she has to do is tell them who and what she wants for the ceremony and reception, keep her appointments, and show up.

I think I might be more excited about it than she is.

One day, I'm not sure when, Tamera overheard me singing *Lift Every Voice and Sing* while vacuuming the carpets. That gave her the "brilliant" idea to ask me to sing it for her retirement ceremony.

I asked if someone would be running a vacuum while I sang, because that's the only way I'd do it.

"I don't sing in public, Sister!" I told her.

She just smiled and said she'll see about having someone run the vacuum while I sing. I'm pretty sure I did not say yes, but I think I'm singing for her.

WHAT IN THE WORLD?!

When I told Hezekiah, he thought it was wonderful — his baby singing one of the most prestigious songs ever written.

"Thank you, sir, for making me feel even more terrified. I appreciate you!"

The Dress

Tamera, the girls, and I went wedding dress shopping. How do I even explain how I feel right now?

I've looked at so many dresses in magazines. A couple of weeks ago, Tamera and I went window shopping...nothing. I knew I didn't want a traditional white gown dripping in lace and bubbles. I like princess-style dresses with wide skirts, but even that didn't quite feel like "me."

Hezekiah has been a true Godly man, honoring my space from the day we met. He makes a point not to cross any lines with his words or gestures before we are legally and biblically married. I've been careful not to wear or do anything that would make it harder for him to keep that vow. On our wedding day, when he sees me, I want him to see a Godly, beautiful woman ready to be his Queen.

The store we visited was a vintage thrift shop — affordable, but far from trashy. Most of their inventory came from movie sets, with costumes from every era. The girls were on a mission to find "princess gowns." I was hoping to find *the* dress — the one I'd dreamed of wearing if I ever got married for real. I knew I'd know it when I saw it.

The salesman was kind and patient, making sure the girls had hats, feathers, and high heels to play with while we browsed. The shop was much bigger inside than it looked from the street, each corner revealing a new style, a different time period.

I saw a couple of dresses that caught my eye and tried them on — but they weren't right.

Then, I turned into the next room.

There it was, in the corner by the window — an off-white eyelet lace gown.

Short sleeves. The perfect neckline — neither too high nor too low — ideal for the pearls Mrs. Johnnes had sent me. The skirt was full but not ballooning, elegant without excess.

I froze, suddenly nervous. What if it didn't fit? What if it cost too much? What if... what if...

Tamera smiled, nodding. "Try it on. It's you."

The girls chimed in, urging me on.

I hesitated — then a warm ray of sunlight spilled through the window, touching the eyelets and making them glow as if the dress had its own light.

In the dressing room, I slipped into it. The first "what if" faded immediately — it fit perfectly. The only alteration needed was a quick hem so it wouldn't drag under my shoes.

When I stepped out, all I heard was a chorus of "Oooohs" and "Aaaahs."

I stood before the mirror in the late-afternoon light. The lace eyelets traced delicate patterns over satin, each stitch whispering promises of patience and new beginnings. The off-the-shoulder neckline framed my collarbone like a quiet smile. The short sleeves brushed my skin like a steadying hand. The skirt flowed from the hips, gliding into a clean line that skimmed the floor.

As Tamera fastened the last satin button, I saw the sunlight filtering through them. For the first time, I didn't see the girl who had survived. I saw the woman who had arrived.

When I turned, tears filled Tamera's eyes. Ruth, Melody, and Esther stared at me as if they were looking at a real-life princess.

The salesman told us the dress had been worn in *My Fair Lady* — and that I looked just like Audrey Hepburn.

But what brought tears to my own eyes was Ruth's voice, soft and sure: "Oh Mommy, you look like an angel."

Melody and Esther echoed, "Yes, you do!"

Tamera nodded in agreement. And just like that, the rest of the "what-ifs" didn't matter anymore.

That night, sitting on my patio, I listened to the frogs and crickets talking to each other. I made a decision.

I called Frank and asked him to come up for a minute.

When he arrived, I told him how happy I was to have him as my big brother — and that I wouldn't have survived without him in my life. Then I asked if he would honor me by walking me down the aisle and giving me away to Hezekiah.

He smiled, hugged me, and said, "Of course. I'd be honored. I couldn't ask for a better sister—or a better man to give you away to."

OSCS(SW) Tamera Smith Jordan

United States Navy

Retired

October 31, 2000

Today, Tamera closed a chapter that had spanned her entire adult life. Her retirement ceremony was the most sacred and moving event I have ever witnessed — in person or on television.

So many people stood to speak about her. I was deeply impressed, because I'd never really known the full scope of her work. One story in particular stood out — how, while serving on one of her ships, she detected an enemy submarine, preventing it from reaching its destination. People she had served under and those who had served under her all spoke of her excellence, integrity, and leadership.

Two moments in the ceremony especially touched me.

First, a group of sailors — all women — stood in every uniform Tamera had worn throughout her career. They folded the flag with precision, passing it down the line until it reached her. Each movement was crisp, every salute deliberate. Tamera then walked over and placed the folded flag into Frank's hands, telling him that without his love and support, she couldn't have served the flag as she had. His quiet tears said everything.

The second moment was when the guest speaker, a distinguished female Captain, approached the podium. Everyone stood in respect. She introduced herself as Tamera's first division officer from their very first duty station — Tamera a young Seaman, and she an Ensign. "We were as mismatched as two different shoes," she laughed. "I was from upstate New York, and Tamera from New Orleans. What a pair we made."

They had remained friends for more than twenty years. She shared stories about their time together and spoke on the history of women in the Navy. She told us about the WAVES—*Women Accepted for Volunteer Emergency Service*—the group formed during World War II to free men for combat roles. Though demobilized after the war, women were finally integrated into the regular Navy in 1948, and the term "WAVES" remained until the mid-1970s.

She spoke of Tamera as a trailblazer—the first Black female Operations Specialist assigned to two different ships. She recounted the submarine detection story from her own perspective. "That night," she said, "all the men on watch knew something was out there, but they couldn't find it. I believe God meant for Tamera to be the one to spot it. The technical explanation would bore you, but just know she found it, she identified it, and she changed the way the men on that crew viewed her… and the way they viewed women in her field."

Then, a young woman sang *Waves of the Navy.* Her voice was so pure and strong, it made me even more nervous about my own part of the program.

Waves of the Navy, there's a ship sailing round the bay,

And she won't slip into port again until the break of day.

So carry on for that gallant ship, and for every hero brave,

Who will find ashore, his man-size chore was done by a Navy WAVE.

When it was time for Tamera to speak, the applause was long and loud. She embraced the Captain for a long moment before stepping to the podium.

Her voice was steady, but I could tell she was holding back tears. She said the Navy had saved her life, and in turn she had committed her service to saving others — whether an entire crew or one struggling sailor barely holding on. The Navy had given her everything she needed, she said, including her husband Frank. That earned a laugh from the crowd.

She left the younger sailors with this wisdom: "Remember, your allegiance is to God first, and to the United States Navy. If you abide by the laws of both, all good things will be added unto you."

She presented Frank and her children with special tokens of appreciation. But then came the surprise — Frank and the children had a gift for her: a clay statue of a female Senior Chief Petty Officer in khakis, binoculars around her neck. Frank said, "The best thing the Navy ever did for me was let me separate… so I could become part of her seabag gear." The inscription read: *You Fought a Good Fight.* This time, Tamera cried openly.

Then it was my turn. I looked at Hezekiah. He gave me that smile and a small nod—just enough to steady my nerves.

I poured every ounce of myself into the song for my sister. Later, Tamera said between me and the pianist, it was a "#1 Top Ten."

It truly was a beautiful day.

"Lift every voice and sing, till earth and heaven

ring.

Ring with the harmony of Liberty.

Let our rejoicing rise, high as the listening skies

Let it resound, loud as the rolling sea."

Someone Exactly Like You...

Somewhere in the next room, laughter and music floated through the air like dandelion seeds. I stayed still, letting the mirror confirm what my heart already knew: I was ready.

Behind me stood Tamera in the most beautiful oyster-pink gown, Melody, Ruth, and Esther in their Cinderella dresses, and Mrs. Johnnes, who I had instructed to be seated in the front row alongside my mother, Samantha, and Ms. Connie.

Mrs. Johnnes prayed:

"Our Father, who art in heaven, hallowed be Thy Name. Father God, we thank You for the privilege of being Your daughters. We intercede right now, in the Name of Your Son Jesus, for Jane. Walk with her, along with Frank, down the aisle today. As You place her in the hands of Hezekiah, bind Yourself around them. Let them feel Your presence so they know You are with them now and will be with them for as long as they allow You to be.

Thank You for the journey Jane has walked to reach this day. Continue to walk with her, let the Holy Spirit teach her, and anoint her from the crown of her head to the soles of her feet. Let her be the helpmeet You intended for Hezekiah and let her teach every child she touches about Your love. In the Name of Jesus, Amen."

After the prayer, every woman in the room had to fix her makeup again. Soon, everyone was gone except Tamera and me.

She smoothed my hair and the orchids and baby's breath clipped to my veil. Wiping the tears from my eyes, she hugged me and said, "It's time, Sissy. Go claim your King."

Hezekiah stood at the front of the chapel with Josiah, David, James, and John at his side.

His parents were already seated. My mother, sister, and Mrs. Johnnes were in place. The musicians played softly.

He tried not to look nervous, tried not to fidget, but he couldn't help it. She wasn't late, yet it felt like he'd been standing there for ten hours. Then the first chords of their chosen song began — not the traditional wedding march, but *Someone Exactly Like You* by Van Morrison.

The ring bearer hurried down the aisle.

Esther followed. When she saw Hezekiah, she stopped, walked up, and handed him a fistful of flower petals.

Melody came next, smiling the entire way, plucking petals one at a time.

Then Ruth — radiant and looking more like her mother every day — walked down the aisle. She smiled at Hezekiah and blew him a kiss. His throat tightened.

Then Tamera stood in the archway. She was so beautiful. It was probably a good thing Frank wasn't the best man, he might have forgotten he wasn't the one getting married. Her boys gave her a big smile and a slow salute.

The music paused, and the soloist began singing *Someone Exactly Like You.*

The room blurred. The chairs, the faces, the rustle of fabric—everything dimmed. All Hezekiah could see was her, standing in the archway.

When Jane stepped into view, he forgot to breathe.

The lace eyelets caught the light like spun silk, patterns dancing over satin that traced her frame. Her slender neck cradled the pearls from Mrs. Johnnes, the bodice resting perfectly, the skirt full at the hips before gliding into a soft, unhurried sweep.

Her hair caught the sunlight, the veil softening her face — but it was her eyes that stopped him cold. Calm. Steady. Locked on his, as though she had been walking toward him her whole life.

Something hot and tight rose in his chest. Not just pride. Not even joy. Something deeper. He'd seen her cry, fight, and sit quietly in thought — but this was her choosing him. Choosing *them.*

Halfway down the aisle, Frank stopped her and signaled for Hezekiah to come get his Queen. He tried not to run, but his feet didn't quite obey.

When he reached her, he stood for a moment and breathed her in. Then he shook Frank's hand, hugged him, and held out his arm for her to take.

As they walked the rest of the way together, he whispered one word: "Forever."

The ceremony passed in a daze. I couldn't take my eyes off him. I remembered the first time those eyes caught me before I fell, at the marketplace, in the park, gazing at the *Silver Moon,* the night he proposed. I knew I'd be looking into them for the rest of my life.

I heard the pastor begin, "Jane Smith Burton, do you take Hezekiah Arnell Jackson..."

"Yes!" I said before he could finish. Hezekiah did almost the same thing.

The pastor laughed. "Are we in a hurry?"

"Yes!" Hezekiah said, to more laughter.

"Then," the pastor said, "I now pronounce you man and wife. You may finish kissing your bride."

Hezekiah didn't wait for him to finish— he kissed me like I had never been kissed before. When he pulled back, all my lipstick was on him.

It was the most beautiful sight I had ever seen.

I whispered, "I pray you kiss me like this for the rest of our lives."

He replied, "Challenge accepted, ma'am." And kissed me again.

"Ladies and gentlemen," the pastor announced, "I present to you Mr. and Mrs. Hezekiah Arnell Jackson. What God has joined together, let no man put asunder."

Epilogue

Silver Moon

The vows were spoken, the rings exchanged, and as Hezekiah kissed me, I felt the world pause. The children clapped, the family cheered, and for just a moment, time itself seemed to bow its head in reverence to the love God had stitched together between us.

That night, instead of jetting off alone, we began our very non-traditional honeymoon at Disney World—with the entire gang in tow. Josiah, David, Hakeem, the girls, everyone. One big family reunion, noisy and full of laughter. Our only rule was simple: no one was allowed to spend the night in *our* room.

We had a wonderful time. A couple of days we slipped away to enjoy events alone while Frank and Tamera entertained the family, and we returned the favor so they could have their own time together. It wasn't the quiet escape most couples imagine, but it was us. A blending of lives and histories. Hezekiah gained little ones to love; I gained grown sons to embrace. It was messy and joyful and absolutely perfect.

On our last night in Orlando, when the bustle of the day had quieted, Hezekiah and I slipped out onto the balcony. The Florida air was warm, the laughter of our family muffled behind closed doors. Hezekiah took my hand and pointed upward.

"Sweetheart, look."

I followed his gaze, past the city lights, past the stars, until my eyes rested on the soft glow hanging in the sky.

"Silver Moon," he whispered.

The words wrapped around me like a promise. I leaned into him, my heart full, and silently thanked God — for the sign, for the man beside me, and for the truth I now carried deep in my spirit: that God always knows what's best for me. Hezekiah and I would walk together, forever and always, beneath His light.

"And we know that God causes all things to work together for good to those who love God, to those who are called according to His purpose."

(Romans 8:28 NIV)

Appendix

The Four Selfs

(Concept, Worth/Value, Identity, Esteem)

While reading this trilogy, what did you think of Janedoah's concept of who she was? Did you notice her growth? Which moments or events showed it most clearly?

Jane's journey began the day her mother chose to name her Janedoah Smith — her parents' way of disguising the fact they'd really named her Jane Doe Smith... "Dead Girl Walking." From birth, she was sent the message she was neither wanted nor loved. She grew up in a home marked by neglect and abandonment, then entered adulthood with abuse layered on top of that early pain.

Because of her childhood and adult experiences, Jane never learned the importance of self-love or self-care. She lacked what I call the **Four Selfs** — something you may recognize in yourself as you read her story:

1. **Self-Concept** – How you see yourself: physically, emotionally, spiritually, and in your own opinion of who you are (your identity). It shapes your confidence and affects how you show up in the world.

2. **Self-Worth/Value** – Do I matter? Am I valuable to myself and to others? Self-worth is often tied to skills, achievements, status, finances, or physical traits — however, real worth is deeper.

3. **Self-Identity** – Knowing God sees every flaw, yet through the blood of Jesus erases them all. If we don't believe this

truth, Satan will whisper that God made a mistake and we must change to be "enough."

4. **Self-Esteem** – Our overall evaluation of ourselves. It includes beliefs ("I am competent" or "I am unworthy") and feelings such as pride, shame, love, or despair.

In Jane's case, the teaching and guidance from Dr. Matthews and Mrs. Johnnes centered on **why** she believed what she did about herself — and on challenging the false voices which had shaped her. She eventually learned God makes no mistakes, and the people who told her otherwise never had her best interests at heart. By the end, Jane had grown to understand:

a) Who she truly was (**self-concept**)

b) Why she was valuable (**self-worth**)

c) That she was made perfect in God's eyes,

and that those who truly loved her would
celebrate her (**self-identity**)

d) That she was important (**self-esteem**)

Repercussions of Parenting Styles
(Specifically Neglectful / Uninvolved)

While reading Dead Girl Walking and Jane's Journey, how do you think Jane's parents' style of parenting influenced how she interacted with her own children – and with Hezekiah?

Research identifies four main parenting styles, each with its own impact not only as children, but as adults interacting with their own children:

1. **Authoritarian** – Strict, controlling, often using corporal punishment to enforce rules. **Children of highly authoritarian parents will more than likely struggle personally, emotionally, spiritually and socially, and may be likely to become authoritarian or permissive parents themselves.**

2. **Authoritative** – The healthiest style: loving but firm, balancing discipline with compassion. Authoritative parents put a lot of effort into maintaining a positive relationship with their children while providing a strict structure and discipline based on love and educating their children concerning their behavior. They take care to validate their children's feelings and take their opinions into consideration. The authoritative parent practices positive discipline by praising good behavior and implementing reward systems to stop undesirable behavior. Research has shown adult children of authoritative parents are most likely to be well-adjusted, responsible, happy and successful. They are more than likely to be authoritative parents.

3. **Permissive (Indulgent)** – Permissive parents (also referred to as indulgent parents) are parents who may be attentive and warm but may not set many rules for their children. They may prioritize being their child's friend over being their parent. Research suggests the children of permissive parents may show higher levels of creativity, and may also feel entitled and be more interested in taking rather than giving in their own relationships. Children raised by permissive parents may become impulsive and lack self-discipline as adults, leading to potential problems in relationships and work environments. They may easily fall into the realm of neglectful / uninvolved parents by being more concerned about their own needs, as opposed to the needs of their children. On the other hand, because of

the absence of parental support, they may lean towards other more responsible adults to satisfy their need for organization, which will give them the tools needed to raise their own children differently.

4. Neglectful / Uninvolved – Neglectful / Uninvolved parents cannot (or will not) devote sufficient - if any - time to meeting the child's needs. This can be as extreme as neglecting to provide food or clothing but it is more often a failure to meet emotional needs or to have a consistent presence in the child's life. They are largely not available in the daily lives of their children and are unlikely to help with everyday needs of their children, such as, homework or support extracurricular activities, problem solving, or everyday health

needs. Uninvolved parents may often be unaware of their child's whereabouts and do not know their children's friends or teachers. Quite often, children of neglectful/uninvolved parents are basically left to raise themselves. There are several reasons why a parent may be uninvolved including a demanding job, financial stresses, mental health issues or substance abuse problems. Children of uninvolved parents often struggle with self-esteem issues, difficulty forming relationships, and are more likely to get caught up in a bad crowd, to try drugs or to experience teenage parenthood. As adults they often find themselves in difficult situations, however, they may also find a way to live a more stable life than their parents, especially when it comes to caring for their own children.

Jane's parents were deliberately neglectful and uninvolved throughout her childhood and into adulthood. Thankfully, she found a safe place with someone who could help her gain the skills she needed to become a healthy, productive adult and parent.

Post-Traumatic Stress Disorder (PTSD)

(Source:

https://www.mayoclinic.org/diseases-conditions/post-traumatic-stress-disorder/symptoms-causes/syc-20355967)

In Jane's Journey and Silver Moon, we learn Hezekiah lives with PTSD. Though he managed his symptoms through therapy, a severe episode while driving an 18-wheeler made him realize he wasn't fully "over" it. He eventually left truck driving and began a new chapter in life.

Post-traumatic stress disorder (PTSD) is a mental health condition caused by an extremely stressful or terrifying event, one in which a person was physically involved in the event or witnessed the event. Symptoms may include flashbacks, nightmares, night terrors, severe anxiety and uncontrollable thoughts about the event.

"In the story what caused Hezekiah to have flashbacks of the accident?"

Intrusive memories

Symptoms of intrusive memories may include:

1. Unwanted, distressing memories of a traumatic event that comes back over and over again.
2. Reliving a traumatic event as if it were happening again, also known as flashbacks.
3. Upsetting dreams or nightmares about a traumatic event.
4. Severe emotional distress or physical reactions to something that reminds you of a traumatic event.

Because PTSD is triggered by attacks on your five senses (smell, taste, hearing, sight, and touch) it is not always easy to avoid. Some

people find ways to avoid attacks by (which
are not always successful):

1. Trying not to think or talk about a
   traumatic event.
2. Staying away from places, activities or
   people that remind you of a traumatic
   event.

Treatment for PTSD

It is important to note not everyone who
experiences trauma develops PTSD, and not
everyone who develops PTSD requires
psychiatric treatment. For some people,
symptoms of PTSD subside or disappear over
time. Others get better with the help of their
support system (family, friends or clergy).
Many people with PTSD need professional
treatment to recover from psychological
distress that can be intense and disabling. It is
important to remember trauma may lead to
severe distress. Distress is not the individual's

fault, and PTSD is treatable. The earlier a person gets treatment, the better chance of recovery.

Psychiatrists and other mental health professionals use various effective and research-proven methods to help people recover from PTSD. Both talk therapy (psychotherapy) and medication provide effective evidence-based treatments for PTSD.

If you or someone you know may be displaying signs of PTSD your best help for yourself or them is to seek medical attention as soon as possible. Talking to your primary care doctor is a good start. They will be able to provide consultations to mental health professionals.

If you have any questions please feel free to contact me, Dr. AudreyAnn C. Moses. I will be happy to guide you in the correct direction.

DR. AUDREYANN C. MOSES

Social Media: Dr. AudreyAnn Moses

Website:

https://www.transitionlifecoach4u.com

Email: neversaycaint@yahoo.com or

audreyannsbooks@yahoo.com

God Bless you and thank you for reading the Dead Girl Walking Trilogy. It has been a pleasure writing for you. Please leave a review on Amazon, Goodreads or leave me a note on my website or email address. I would love to hear from you.

You are welcome to browse my collection of books available on Amazon at Amazon https://www.amazon.com/~/e/B08CXBGQ8 3

Or if you would like an autographed copy you can order any of my books on my website at https://transitionlifecoach4u.com/order-books. You will always find my newest releases and a special surprise available on my website.

I am available to book clubs interested in reviewing my books. Just send me a note on

my website of email me at
audreyannsbooks@yahoo.com.

    I look forward to hearing from you
soon.

Love

Dr. Audreyann

Silver Moon is the final book in the Dead Girl Walking Trilogy.

I hear you asking when's the next Hezekiah and Jane book coming out. Look for them in Book 3 of the Saved By Grace Series. I anticipate a publishing date around October 2026. Don't miss the announcement. Sign up for email notifications at

https://transitionlifecoach4u.com

Echoes Under the Silver Moon

Step into the voices of those who journeyed through Silver Moon before its release. In this collection of advanced reader reflections, you'll find heartfelt impressions, honest feedback, and the lasting resonance the story left on their hearts.

These echoes capture the wonder, the questions, and the inspiration that arose beneath the glow of the Silver Moon. From whispered praises to thoughtful critiques, these early voices offer a glimpse into how the book touches the soul — illuminating the path for future readers to follow.

Dr. Rhonda Lawson: *Silver Moon is a warm, faith-forward, and emotionally satisfying conclusion to Jane's arc from Dead Girl Walking. It is an inspirational blend of women's fiction and generational healing. When I first met Jane in Dead Girl Walking, she was a woman who struggled to find herself. In Silver Moon, I felt her strength,* *confidence, and courage. Thank you, Dr. AudreyAnn, for showing the world what it means to surround yourself with a tribe that speaks life into you instead of darkness. Silver Moon is a well-written love letter to every girl seeking love and self-worth.*

Donna Coats: *Silver Moon by AudreyAnn Moses is the third book following the life of "Janedoah Smith Burton". It shows remarkable spiritual growth despite the emotional, mental, and physical abuse endured throughout her childhood and adult married life. In spite of Jane's failures and suffering, she emerged victorious with renewed faith and found true love in the arms of Hezekiah.*

Dennis Moll: *Insightful and well written. The Bible verses at the beginning of each chapter are inspiring. The story teaches what faith, patience and love can do to help heal the soul. Hezekiah's story was well told.*

Dr. Jacqueline Cox: Silver Moon is heartfelt, inspiring, and full of God's grace. It's the kind of story that stays with you long after you finish.

Mark Webb, Sr.: I love following the journey of Jane. Her spiritual growth, faith and life are inspiring. There is a Jane in all of us.

Ms. Queenie Clem: A Silver Moon is a moving story of healing, faith, and second chances. With raw honesty and deep emotion, it offers hope and reminds readers that with God, no heart is beyond restoration.

Shirley Johnson: Jane was the character I identified with the most. She experienced the same hurts, pains, abuse, and disappointments I experienced. I love the fact that she overcame as she listened to Mrs. Johnnes and her Jesus papers.

ABOUT THE AUTHOR

Dr. AudreyAnn C. Moses
Certified Christian Life Coach | Mental Wellness Counselor | Bestselling Author | US Navy (Retired)

I am dedicated to empowering individuals to achieve personal and professional growth. With a deep passion for community development, I actively participate in programs that foster meaningful transformation.

As an experienced workshop and program facilitator, I bring insight and encouragement to those seeking positive change. My work extends beyond coaching. I am a five-time bestselling author and recipient of multiple literary awards. My portfolio includes eight published novels, and professional magazine articles focused on personal growth, self-care, and transformation.

To connect with me please visit
https://transitionlifecoach4u.com

I am a multi-book award winning bestselling author. I have written eight books, and a multitude of magazine articles. I have also had the privilege of co-authoring seven anthologies.

My husband, Leonard (also a Navy Vietnam Veteran), and I live in Greenwood, South Carolina. We have four adult children, ten grandchildren, and two great-grandsons — life experiences that inspire my stories about Christian family dynamics, love, and devotion to one another and to God.

Connect with me:

- Website – For coaching sessions, workshops, speaking engagements, and Autographed copies of my books.

- Amazon Author Page – To explore my novels.

- Coaching & workshops: neversaycaint@yahoo.com

- Book tours, signings, and orders: audreyannsbooks@yahoo.com

- 🔗 <u>Linktree</u> – To access all my platforms in one place.